NEWTON AND CURIE

TAKE FLIGHT!

DANIEL KIRK

Abrams Books for Young Readers · New York

For Howard

The art for this book was digitally drawn and painted in Photoshop.

Cataloging-in-Publication Data has been applied for
and may be obtained from the Library of Congress.

ISBN 978-1-4197-4963-6

Text and illustrations © 2023 Daniel Kirk
Edited by Howard W. Reeves
Book design by Heather Kelly and Natalie Padberg Bartoo

Printed and bound in China
10 9 8 7 6 5 4 3 2 1

Abrams Books for Young Readers are available at special discounts when purchased in quantity for
premiums and promotions as well as fundraising or educational use. Special editions can also be
created to specification. For details, contact specialsales@abramsbooks.com or the address below.

Abrams® is a registered trademark of Harry N. Abrams, Inc.

ABRAMS The Art of Books
195 Broadway, New York, NY 10007
abramsbooks.com

urie was sitting under a tree when a baby bird bounced off her head. "Whoa," she cried. "You've fallen right out of your nest!"

"I didn't fall," the little bird cheeped. "I flew. Or at least I tried!"

"Look out, here come my brothers and sisters," the bird cried.

"I've got you," Curie said, and she dashed to catch the babies
before they landed on the soft grass.

"Thanks," called Mother Robin, "but you didn't need to do that. This is how my fledglings learn to fly!"

"Wow," Curie said. "Can you teach me, too?"

Father Robin cocked his head. "Squirrels can't fly! And it's not safe for you to jump out of the trees. You're too heavy, and you have no wings."

Newton heard the commotion and slipped out of a classroom window. He often hid at the back of the class, learning along with the children.

"Newton," Curie called to her big brother,
"Mr. Robin said squirrels can't fly!"

"Well, just think of all the great things
squirrels can do," Newton said.

"But I really want to fly," Curie said, disappointed. "I want to see the world from up above the trees, like the birds. I'll bet it's wonderful!"

"I'm going to do an experiment," she said to herself, looking for feathers that had fallen to the ground. "If I find enough, I can make myself some wings, just like a bird."

It took a few days for Curie to gather enough feathers
and string to create her own set of wings.

She strapped them over her arms. Then she jumped
up and down, flapping like a bird. But she did not fly!

The little robins couldn't help but laugh when they
saw the squirrel. "Just you wait," Curie cried.

Later, Curie watched children taking turns jumping on a trampoline. It almost looked like they were flying into the air.

"Maybe if I can get a little higher in the air to begin with, then I'll be able to catch a breeze with my wings and fly. If only I had a trampoline!"

The next day Curie found a big, spongy mushroom.
"I'll bet this will help me spring into the air," she said.

She poked some sticks into the ground beside the mushroom
so Newton could measure how high she was able to go.

Curie jumped and jumped, flapping
her wings as hard as she could. "You got
a little higher that time," Newton said,
"but you're not really flying."

"I guess jumping high and flying aren't nearly the same thing," Curie said sadly. "And a mushroom isn't a trampoline."

"Let's think about it," Newton said to his little sister. "What exactly is flight?"

"Hmm . . . flight is what happens when an object moves through the air on its own," Curie answered.

"That's right," Newton replied. "It's all about the air. Air is a gas we can't see or taste or touch, but we know it's there! It seems to me that the birds use the air, somehow, to fly. It's not just the muscles in their wings."

Curie said, "But gravity pulls air down, just like it does every other thing. What we need is a way to defy gravity!"

The next day, Curie saw a group of children toss something from a classroom window. "It's just a piece of folded-up paper," she exclaimed. "But it sure can move!"

Curie found some paper to do her experiments. "Look at this,"
she said to her big brother. "I'll take a piece of paper and
throw it into the air. Watch what happens!"

"Not much," Newton said.

Curie nodded. "Now I'll ball up some paper and
throw it. We'll see what happens then!"

"It goes a little farther,"
Newton said.

"Now watch this," Curie said, as she folded some paper
into an airplane and tossed it into the breeze.

"It's really flying!" Newton exclaimed.

Curie nodded. "I think it's more like gliding, because it doesn't have the power to stay up on its own for long.

"When you fold the paper this way, the shape is simple and sleek. And the more force you use to throw it, the faster and the farther it goes."

"So for you to do what the paper plane does, you would need to wear your lightest clothes," Newton said. "And we would need a big force to push you into the air."

"Maybe it's time to give my feathered wings away," Curie said. "You could put them in the classroom for the kids to find. Then we can make a new design!"

"It seems to me," Newton said, "that staying in the air depends on what they call air pressure."

"The way these glider wings are shaped, the air will move a bit faster over the top, and that will make the pressure on the top less than on the bottom. That should give you more lift!"

"And that will keep me in the air longer? I'll bet you learned that in school," Curie said.

"Yes! So come on," Newton said. "I know just where to get some materials we can borrow! And you can help."

The squirrels found some thin wooden strips, glue, and rubber bands from bins in the classroom. "School looks like fun," Curie said.

Newton nodded. "It is!"

Newton and Curie got to work building
a glider based on their design.

They also made their very own catapult! "We've got a lever and a fulcrum,"
Newton said. "That's all you need for this simple machine."

Curie put on her lightest clothes to wear for the flight. "This is great," Curie said. "And the more force you put on the lever, the farther I'll sail!"

"All ready?" Newton cried. "Three, two, one, *TAKEOFF!*" Then he jumped onto the end of the lever.

"Look at you go!" Newton cried.

Curie shot into the air, and her heart beat with joy.

It wasn't bad for a first try, but down she went,
tumbling to the ground. "Whoa!" she hollered.

The science squirrels built a new glider, with longer wings. "Maybe these will give me more lift," Curie said.

"And I have an idea of how to launch you better, too!" Newton said.

They planted the end of a forked branch in the ground near the field and tied some rubber bands together until they had one long, stretchy strap.

"When I use force to pull this back," Newton said, "energy is stored in the rubber bands. The energy gets released when I let go, and that's why this slingshot will help get you airborne."

"I'm ready," Curie said.

"Three, two, one, *TAKEOFF!*" Newton shouted,
and he let go of the rubber band.

Curie sailed through the air, and this time she
flew higher and farther.

But she soon landed with a thump.
"WHOA!" she cried, as Newton ran
to the rescue.

"I think you pulled too hard, so I went too fast," Curie said. "That's why I crashed like that. I guess I'll never be able to fly like a bird."

"You were gliding," Newton said, "and that's almost as good as flying!"

Curie sighed. "I know I'm not really flying if I can't do it completely on my own. But I sure would love to stay in the air for a little longer."

"Would you like some help?" asked the four young robins, who were better fliers every day. "We have an idea! Can you find four long pieces of string and get your glider up into the tree?"

So Newton and Curie patched up their glider, and fixed strings to the wings and tail as the birds instructed. They used a pulley to hoist it high into the branches.

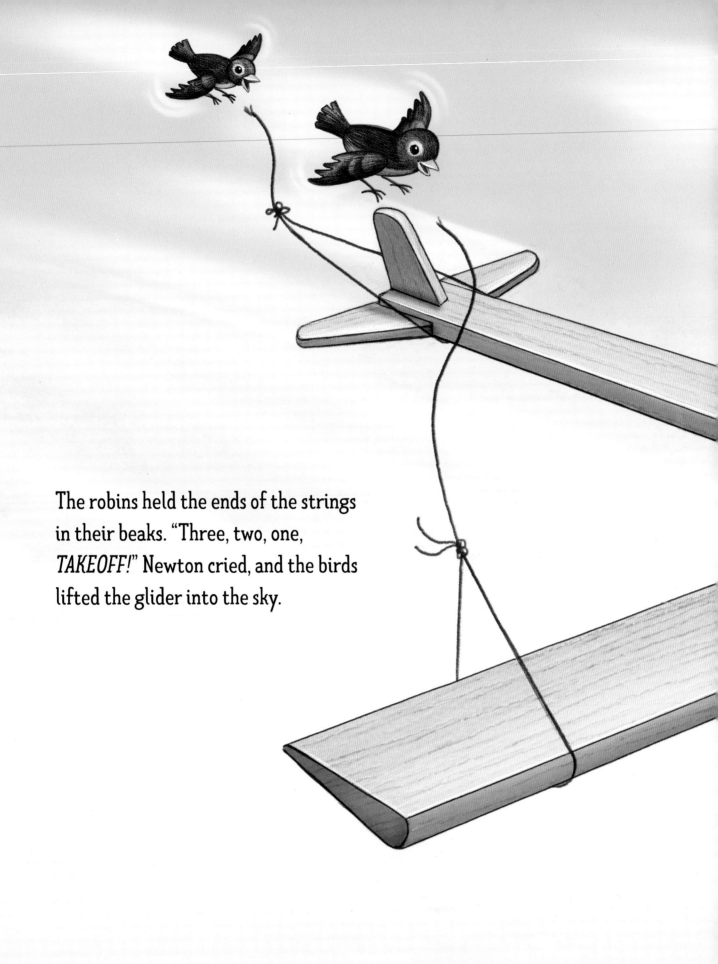

The robins held the ends of the strings in their beaks. "Three, two, one, *TAKEOFF!*" Newton cried, and the birds lifted the glider into the sky.

"Look how high I can go," Curie cried,
"with a little help from my friends!"

And when the birds let go of the strings, Curie
glided on the currents of air, and she sailed
farther than she'd ever gone before.

"So a squirrel might not be able to fly," Newton said as Curie safely landed, "but with a little help, she sure can glide!"

"She sure can," said Curie. "With a little help from our friends, and a little science."

"You really did it," Newton said. "I'm so proud of you!"

Curie grinned. "Let's sneak our old gliders into the classroom.
And let's stay awhile! I think I'm ready to go to school, like you."

And in the classroom, the very next day . . .

"Look at these little models we found.
Who do you think made them?" asked
one of the students.

"I wish I had a glider big enough
for me," said her classmate.
"Wouldn't it be great to fly?"

AUTHOR'S NOTE

I love to watch the squirrels in my yard scamper across the ground and up the trees. When I leave nuts in a dish, a squirrel will slowly creep up and snatch one. Then it will scurry up a tree, jumping from limb to limb.

Squirrels are skilled jumpers, but can they fly? Curie needs a glider and the help of her flying friends to ride the winds, but there are in fact real "flying" squirrels. They use the thin skin, called a membrane, that spreads between their front and back legs to glide from branch to branch in tall trees. They can travel much farther than regular squirrels do if they merely jump. However, flying squirrels aren't really flying either; they are gliding long distances through the air. Birds and bats can glide through the air, too, but by beating their wings they can stay aloft and truly fly.

GLOSSARY

In *Newton and Curie Take Flight!*, the science squirrels learn about many new things, including air currents, air pressure, and lift. With the understanding they gain from observation and experiments about what it takes to fly, they achieve things most of us can only dream of!

AIR is the invisible gas that surrounds Earth. It's mostly made of oxygen and nitrogen, and animals and plants need air to survive!

AIR CURRENTS are wind moving in a certain direction, like water flowing in a river.

AIR PRESSURE is caused by the gases that make up air. The gases are made of tiny particles called molecules, and these molecules have weight. They press down on whatever is below. Warm air has lower pressure, and cool air has higher pressure.

A **CATAPULT** or **SLINGSHOT** is a machine that works because one kind of energy is converted to another kind, and then transferred from one object to another. Potential energy is stored in the rubber band when it is pulled back on a catapult. When the band is released, the object that is shot out of the catapult uses the energy that was stored in the bands, and it flies through the air.

GRAVITY is an invisible force that pulls objects toward each other. Earth's gravity is what keeps you on the ground and what makes things fall.

A **LEVER AND FULCRUM** is a simple machine where a lever is placed so that its middle sits atop a fulcrum. The fulcrum is the place where the lever pivots (goes up and down). The load goes on one end of the lever. When pressure is added at the other end, the fulcrum helps raise up the load, like on a seesaw.

LIFT works when the wings of an aircraft are shaped so that air on the top of the wing is forced to move faster than the air below the wing. Faster air makes for lower air pressure. If the pressure on the top of the wing is lower than the pressure beneath the wing, the force will lift the wing higher.

A **PULLEY** is a simple machine made by looping a rope or cable over a wheel and is most often used to lift a heavy object. When you pull down on the near end of the rope, it creates an upward pull on the far end to which the object is tied. This makes the job easier!

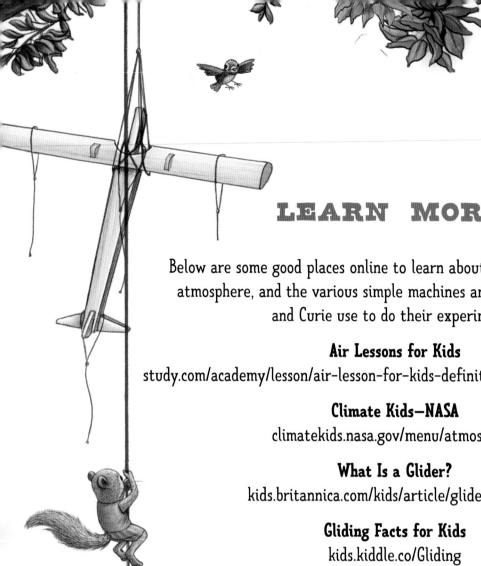

LEARN MORE!

Below are some good places online to learn about flight, as well as our atmosphere, and the various simple machines and tools that Newton and Curie use to do their experiments.

Air Lessons for Kids
study.com/academy/lesson/air-lesson-for-kids-definition-properties-facts.html

Climate Kids—NASA
climatekids.nasa.gov/menu/atmosphere

What Is a Glider?
kids.britannica.com/kids/article/glider/400108

Gliding Facts for Kids
kids.kiddle.co/Gliding

How Do Planes Fly?
youtube.com/watch?v=wFTHh-6jIT8

How Airplanes Fly, for Kids
youtube.com/watch?v=ABhgenHCxGA

What Is a Pulley?
dkfindout.com/uk/science/simple-machines/pulleys

Design Squad: Nate's Slingshot—PBS Kids
youtube.com/watch?v=ikTmPOqTC10

Slingshot Physics
real-world-physics-problems.com/slingshot-physics.html

How Does a Catapult Work?
kids.kiddle.co/Catapult